www.randomhouse.com/kids
www.universalstudios.com

Library of Congress Cataloging-in-Publication Data

Loehr, Mallory.
Babe : a little pig goes a long way / by Mallory C. Loehr ; illustrated by Christopher Moroney ; based on the character Babe created by Dick King-Smith.
p. cm.
SUMMARY: Babe the pig relates his own story as proof that you can do anything if you set your mind to it.
"Beginner books."
ISBN 0-375-80110-3 (trade) — ISBN 0-375-90110-8 (lib. bdg.)
[1. Pigs—Fiction. 2. Animals—Fiction. 3. Stories in rhyme.] I. Moroney, Christopher, ill. II. Title. PZ8.3.L8245Bab 1999 [E]—dc21 98-30342

Printed in the United States of America 10 9 8 7 6 5 4 3 2 1

BABE
The Sheep Pig™

A Little Pig
Goes a Long Way

illustrated by Christopher Moroney

adapted by Mallory Loehr
from the motion picture screenplay
written by George Miller & Chris Noonan

based on *Babe: The Gallant Pig* by Dick King-Smith

BEGINNER BOOKS®

A Division of Random House, Inc.

I am Babe. I'm a pig.
But not just any kind.
I'm a new kind of pig
that's not easy to find.

When I was small,

I was the prize

in a contest called

"Guess This Pig's Size."

I was held by big hands,
turned this way and that.
I was very unhappy.
I just sat and sat.

Then the Boss picked me up.

He looked into my eyes.

Then he spoke—and his guess

was exactly my size!

He guessed that good guess,

and the next thing I knew...

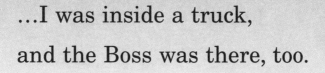

...I was inside a truck,
and the Boss was there, too.

I came to the farm
where I'm living now.

I met...

...chickens

and dogs

and a horse
and a cow...

...and a cat

and some sheep

and a duck

and three mice.

(The mice like to sing,

which can be quite nice.)

This dog is my mom.

The Boss calls her Fly.

I want to be like her.

I work hard and try.

But Mom told me, "Babe,
you are only a pig.
Your job is to stay here
and eat and grow big."

"I'm sorry," she said.
"But that's just the way
things are on the farm—
and that's how they'll stay."

Then the Boss said, "Here, Pig."
And I think that he knew
the thing that I wanted
so badly to do.

That's how I got started

at herding the sheep.

I talk to them nicely.

I don't bark or growl deep.

I say to them, "Madames,
you're looking so fine.
Please do me a favor
and walk in a line."

The sheep are my friends.
They all do what I ask.

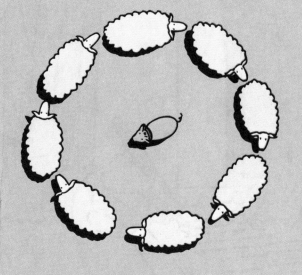

They quickly and quietly
finish each task.

The Boss signed me up
for the sheepdog contest.

Then Mom told me, "Babe,
go and get a good rest."

That night as I lay
all alone in my bed,
I heard a soft voice,
and here's what it said:
"The world can't be changed
by one little pig.
And you will be eaten
when you've gotten big."

It was Duchess the cat.

She purred as she spoke.

"It's the truth, Pig,"

she added. "It isn't a joke."

I talked to my friend
Ferdinand the duck.
He said, "You're a pig
who is down on his luck."

He said to me, "Babe,
pigs have rights, too.
So what do *you* want?
That's what you should do."
Can you guess what I did?
I'll give you one guess.

You're right! I went
and I won that contest!
So Duchess was wrong.
I *did* change my fate.
I went and I acted.
I didn't just wait.
Yes, a little pig
can go a long way
from where he starts out
and from where he might stay.

'Cause you don't have to think
that's the way that things are.
You can think, you can *say,*
"Let's take this world far—
and make it much better
than it is right now!"
You can change the world,
you just have to know how:

Be kind to all creatures,
the shy and the bold,

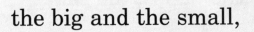

the big and the small,

and the young and the old...

...the happy, the sad,

the good and the bad,

and even be nice

to the ones that get mad.

Chase every rainbow.
Go down every stream.
Follow your heart.
Follow your dream.

That's what I have learned
and what I've told you,

so *you* can go out

and change the world, too!